Will and the
Gold Chase

by JOHN GRANT
illustrated by SARA SILCOCK

Ladybird Books

Camilla had a beautiful gold pendant that she loved very much. It was a present from her uncle, Governor Broadside, and she wore it everywhere she went.

One day, she wore it to go boating, but the chain broke and the pendant fell into the sea. Camilla was very unhappy. She was so upset that Governor Broadside offered a reward.

Jimbo, *originally a stowaway, but Captain Roger allowed him to join the crew as ship's boy*

Flashfork, *ship's cook. He is no master chef but the crew rarely complain; he's a hot-tempered man, armed with a cutlass and a rolling pin!*

Anne, *the daughter of Bessie, landlady at the inn on Pirate Island. She is a fearless pirate and loves to take part in Darkshark's adventures whenever she can*

Spinoza, *the mischievous ship's monkey and* **Popsy**, *Captain Roger's faithful and very talkative parrot*

On the large island of Sabatina, somewhere in the Tropical Sea, lives Governor Broadside with his sister Aunt Prudence and niece Camilla.

Life is never quiet for the Governor and his men as they try to keep law and order in the territory. The seas are full of pirates, pirate ships and pirate adventures, with Captain Roger, Bo'sun Will and the crew of the Darkshark *constantly pitting their wits against their arch enemies, Captain Foul and the crew of the* Barracuda.

British Library Cataloguing in Publication Data
Grant, John, *1930-*
    Will and the gold chase.
    I. Title   II. Silcock, Sara
    823'.914[J]
    ISBN 0-7214-1309-9

First edition

Published by Ladybird Books Ltd Loughborough Leicestershire UK
Ladybird Books Inc Auburn Maine 04210 USA

® LEGO is a registered trademark belonging to the LEGO Group and is used here
  by special permission.
© LEGO GROUP MCMXC
© LADYBIRD BOOKS LTD MCMXC
Printed in England (3)

Fishermen tried to find the pendant with hooks and lines. Others used nets. Pearl divers came from a far-off island. They found several pearls... but no pendant.

The crew of the *Darkshark* heard about the reward. But they were busy pirates. They had no time to look for a lost pendant.

Bo'sun Will felt sorry for Camilla. He had met her when the pirates once captured the Governor's ship and he liked her a lot.

"If only I could find the pendant," he thought to himself. Will didn't care about the reward, he just wanted to make Camilla happy again.

Darkshark was anchored in a quiet bay. It was almost night when suddenly the look-out cried, "Sail Ho!" A small boat was approaching. It was a fishing boat, with a patched red sail.

Flashfork, the cook, knocked on the Captain's cabin door. "We're right out of fish, Cap'n," he said. "We'll need to buy in some supplies."

Captain Roger enjoyed fish for his supper, so he took out the ship's cash box. He kept its gold key hidden in a secret compartment in his wooden leg.

The Captain was just about to put the key in the lock when Spinoza, the ship's monkey, jumped up. He snatched the key and ran on deck. The Captain, the cook and all the crew gave chase.

Spinoza, clutching the key, ran up the rigging and skidded to the end of a yard-arm. Will scrambled after him.

He almost had him by the tail but Spinoza jumped over the water... and landed in the fishing boat.

The pirates shouted after the boat. But it had disappeared into the darkness.

"Hoist the sails!" cried Captain Roger. "Raise the anchor! We must catch that fishing boat."

"In the dark?" said Will. "We don't even know where it's going."

"We don't need a key," said Rummy. "I'll shoot the box open with one of the cannon. Don't you think that's a good idea?"

But nobody did.

"Wait!" cried Will. "Where do fishing boats usually go? Why, to the fish market, with their catch... to Port Royal. That's where we'll find that monkey. And the key."

"Pirates can't just sail into Port Royal," said Rummy.

"In disguise, they can," said Will.

The pirate ship set sail for Port Royal. But she was no longer *Darkshark*. The new name painted on was *Skylark*. Flags were hung from the masts and rigging. The crew were washed and shaved and they wore their best clothes. The Captain wore a handsome white wig and an elegant cloak to hide his wooden leg. Three of the pirates played fiddle, flute and drum on deck.

"Remember," said Captain Roger, "you are *not* pirates. You are passengers. And you are very respectable."

The look-out shouted, "Port Royal! Dead ahead!" The flags fluttered. The music played. The pirates waved to the people on the quay. And the *Skylark* sailed into Port Royal.

SKYLARK

There were dozens of fishing boats in the harbour. There were white sails. And brown. And red. But not one of the red sails was patched.

Will and Jimbo took one of the ship's dinghies and rowed among the fishing boats. They spoke to the fishermen.

"Is there another boat?

With a red patched sail?" Will asked.

"Oh yes," said one of the fishermen, "that's Old Binnacle's boat. He doesn't come to Port Royal. He sells his fish to the islanders."

It was late when Will and Jimbo rowed back to the *Skylark*. Rummy and Captain Roger were on deck. A full moon was rising.

"Captain!" said Will.

"Sh!" said the Captain. He turned his head from side to side. His nose twitched. "Gold! Gold!" he muttered. "I can smell gold. The gold key. It isn't far away. I can smell it."

"But, Captain..." began Will.

"Don't interrupt," said Rummy. "It's the gold-sniffing. It comes upon him at full moon."

"But, Cap..." began Will again.

The Captain wasn't listening. He walked down the gangplank and strode along the quay. Rummy, Will and Jimbo followed. Close behind were Flashfork and some of the crew.

The Captain sniffed and snuffled. He walked faster and faster. Along the quay, past the warehouses and into the fishmarket. It was dark in the shadows, but Captain Roger raced on. The others came behind. They dodged around baskets of fish. They leapt over barrels of oysters.

"Not far now!" cried the Captain, and he ran slap! bang! into a stack of barrels.

The barrels tumbled in all directions. So did the Captain's wig, hat and cloak. His disguise was ruined.

"Halt! In the name of the Governor!" came a voice.

"Yikes! A patrol!" cried Rummy. "Run, lads! They'll recognise the Captain."

The soldiers stormed into the fishmarket. The officer in charge fell over a barrel. The soldiers fell over the officer. And in seconds, the patrol lay piled in a heap among fallen barrels and spilt fish.

"Back to the ship!" cried Captain Roger. "Flashfork! Grab that barrel! At least we'll have fish for breakfast."

The crew jumped aboard ship. Ropes were cast off. Sails were unfurled. And by the time the patrol reached the quay, the *Skylark* was gone.

Will told the Captain about Old Binnacle. "I tried to tell you earlier, but you wouldn't listen," he explained.

They changed course immediately and headed towards the islands. Before long, they saw a fishing boat. It had a red patched sail. "Binnacle, ahoy," hailed Captain Roger.

Darkshark came alongside the fishing boat and Will and the Captain jumped aboard. "We just want our monkey," said Will.

"Monkey?" said Old Binnacle. "I haven't got a monkey."

At the sound of Will's voice, Spinoza, who had been feeling rather homesick, leapt out from his hiding place and jumped onto the rail. Captain Roger made a grab at him... and lost his balance. With a loud splash they both fell into the sea. The fishermen and pirate crew couldn't help laughing.

Old Binnacle took up a boat hook and pulled Captain Roger aboard by his collar. The Captain held Spinoza in one hand and the precious key in the other.

"Well! Well! Bless my soul," said the old fisherman.

They climbed back on board the *Darkshark*. The Captain put the key back into the secret compartment in his wooden leg. Then he put on some dry clothes. Flashfork opened the barrel of fish for supper.

Will picked out a very big fish for himself, but as he cut it open something glittered inside. It was the gold pendant. No one else had seen it so Will put it in his pocket. The Captain's nose had been right. There *was* gold in the fishmarket after all.

As they sat down to supper the
Captain's nose started to twitch again.
"Gold," he sniffed. "I can smell gold."
Then he sneezed loudly.

"You're just catching
a cold," said Will,
pushing the pendant
deep into his
pocket.

Later that evening, Will sat on his bunk and thought hard. He was a pirate. Governor Broadside would never give *him* a reward.

So he wrapped the pendant in a small parcel and addressed it to Camilla at Fort Sabre. He drew a small anchor on the back. The anchor tattooed on his arm.

At first light, when the other pirates were asleep, Will

rowed ashore. He gave the package to an errand boy and asked him to deliver it to Camilla, at Fort Sabre. He hoped that the pendant would reach her safely.

And it did. As soon as Camilla saw the anchor on the package, she knew who had found her pendant. And from then on she was always most careful to look after it — especially when going boating!

THE TREASURE ISLANDS

Darkshark,
Captain Roger's ship

JOHN SILVER
ISLAND

THE TROPICAL SEA

FORT SABRE

PORT ROYAL

SABATINA

FENZANCE

PIRATE'S
HAT
ISLAND

SHARK ISLAND

ISLAND OF FOGS